Ellie the Elephant has a Sleep Study

by Christie Beckwith

Copyright © 2014, 2023 by Christie Beckwith. All rights reserved.
ISBN 9781499127690

For my mom,
who has always been my superhero.

Helloooo there!
My name is Ellie the Elephant.
I haven't told anyone yet, but
I'm a superhero in training!

Today, I went to the doctor because my mom heard me snore in my sleep.
I bet you're wondering how it sounds when an elephant snores in her sleep...

It sounds kind of like,
"Barrooomshoooo!"

The doctor told my mom we would need a <u>sleep study</u> to gather more information.

I was a little bit scared until my mom reminded me that I'm her brave superhero!

The night of my sleep study, I packed an overnight bag with my pillow, jammies, favorite toy, and bedtime story.

"Don't forget your toothbrush and toothpaste!" said my mom.

When we arrived at the sleep lab, we made sure to knock on the door three times.

"KNOCK, KNOCK, KNOCK!"

A nice lady answered the door.
Her name was Sheila. She asked my mom
the secret password. It was my birthday!

Then she showed us to our room.

I was surprised there were two beds.
I got to sleep in my very own bed!

While my mom filled out paperwork,
Sheila asked me to change into my pj's.
When we were ready we opened up the door.
Sheila measured my <u>vital signs</u>:

HEART RATE	96 bpm
BLOOD PRESSURE	101/70
HEIGHT	132 cm
WEIGHT	57.6 kg
TEMPERATURE	37 °c

Then she brought in a cart that had all sorts of colorful wires, stickers, and some interesting piles of goop!

She called the wires <u>electrodes</u>.

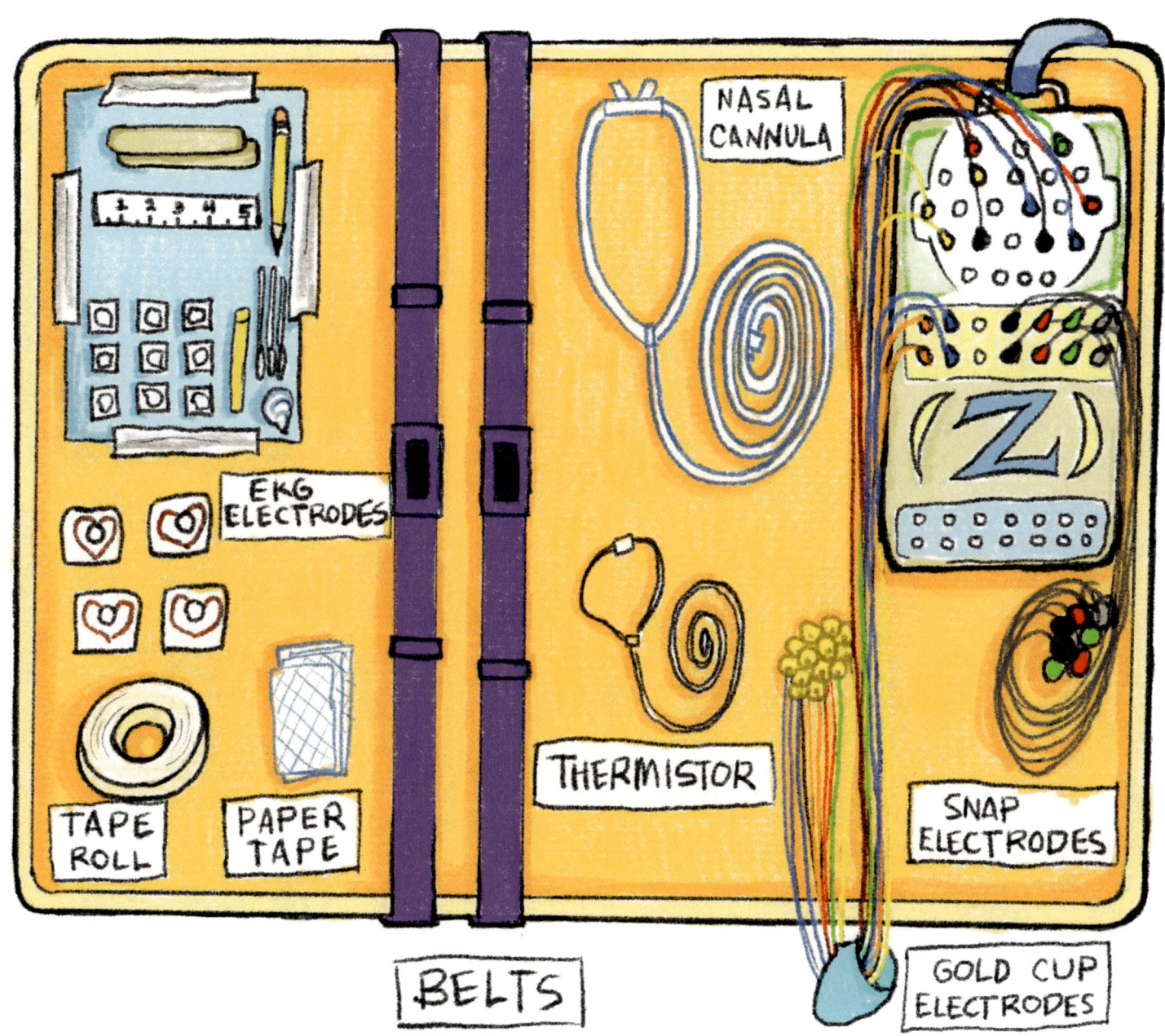

The wires were placed all over!
Most of them were on my face and head.
I felt like I had a new hairdo!

Sheila started to explain everything she was doing and told me she would be able to see my brainwaves to tell if I was awake or asleep!

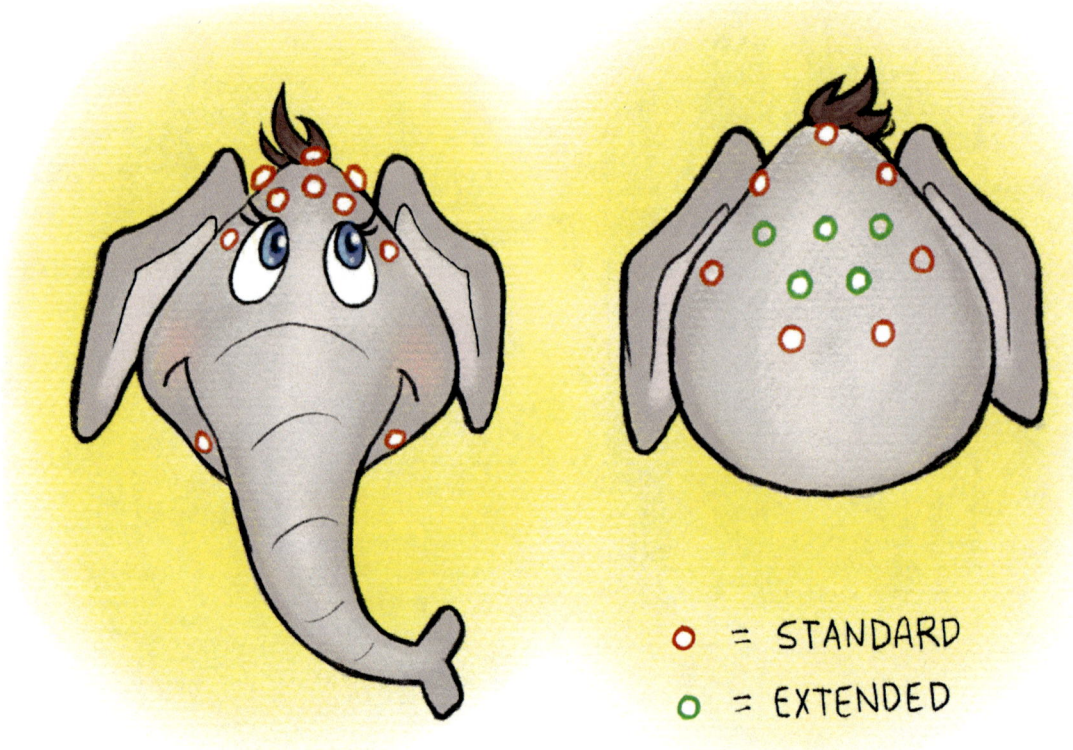

○ = STANDARD
○ = EXTENDED

Wire placement on the head and face

I had some wires on my legs and a few to monitor my heartbeat. I got to wear two belts - one on my tummy and one close to my heart to monitor how I breathed.

I also had a <u>snore microphone</u> to pick up my cool snoring noises.

Then I got a sensor with a red light on my finger that showed the doctors what my oxygen levels were.

The last thing Sheila placed on me was a sensor
to monitor my breathing from my nose.
It was called a <u>cannula</u>.

She warned me that it would tickle a little.
It really tickled, but then
it just felt like I had a mustache!

Once everything was taped on, I got concerned…

"Uh-oh," I said.
"I just realized I have to go to the bathroom."
Sheila explained that I could bring the wirebox
with me. "What a relief," I said.

I was finally ready for bed as Sheila helped me arrange the wires so I would be comfortable.

"Yawwnnbarrooom!"

I was beat!
The sensors felt so weird, but soon I was too tired to notice, and I drifted off to sleep.

I had crazy dreams that night!
I dreamt I was a robot, Frankenstein, a mummy, a lab rat, and astronaut, and then a superhero.

"Wake up, my little superhero," said Mom.

"It's over already?" I said as I yawned. "I can't believe how quickly our sleepover went!"

Sheila explained to my mom that the results would be available soon.

She removed all the goop, stickers, and sensors from me.

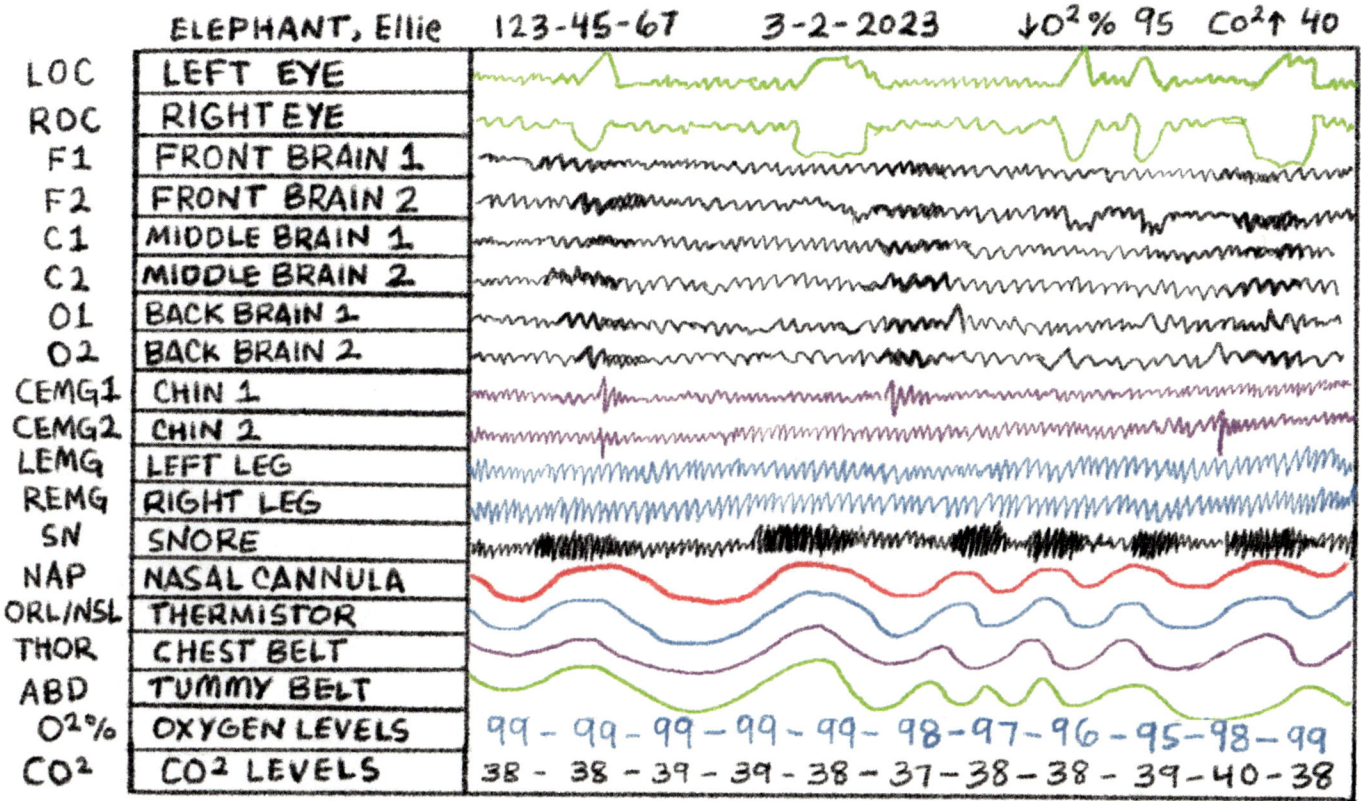

She even let me take home
a <u>screenshot</u> of my sleep study!

"I can't wait to show this to all my friends!" I said.

THE END

For more information on sleep or to find an accredited sleep lab you can visit the National Sleep Foundation Website at:

http://sleepfoundation.org/

This book is available on Kindle through amazon.com.

Glossary of Terms:

Cannula: A sensor with two short prongs that are placed in the nose that picks up the airflow changes in your breathing patterns.

Electrodes: The wires that are used to send the signals from your body to the computer screen where the sleep technologist and doctors can see it.

Screenshot: A copy of the computer screen that shows all of the signals the technologist looks at during your study.

Sleep Lab: The facility where you will have a sleep study. Some sleep labs are in hospitals or hotels, and some sleep labs are in independent buildings.

Sleep Study: A study that records your brain waves, breathing patterns, and muscle movements to determine if you have trouble sleeping.

Sleep Technologist (sleep tech): The staff in the sleep lab that prepares you for your sleep study, monitors your study, and takes the wires off in the morning.

Snore microphone: A small sensor, placed on the side of the neck, that picks up the vibrations from talking, snoring, and chewing or grinding your teeth while you sleep.

Thermistor: A different type of breath sensor that monitors your breathing patterns by sensing the difference in temperatures when you breathe in (inhale) versus when you breathe out (exhale).

Vital Signs: Different measurements such as height, weight, blood pressure, heart rate, and breathing rate that help the tech know that you are healthy enough to have your study.

Acknowledgements

Thank you so much to Damian Bartlett for helping me name Ellie.

Thank you to Sheila Rubino for allowing me to use your likeness as the sleep technician in this book.

Finally, I want to thank all of my fellow sleep technicians at Boston Children's Hospital for implementing such amazing and creative methods to make the complex setup as enjoyable as possible for the kids and their parents.

Made in United States
Orlando, FL
27 December 2023